To The Jackson County Libraries

Happy Sleuthing!

Dave

My name is Seymour Sleuth. I am the greatest
detective in the world. With my faithful assistant
and photographer, Abbott Muggs, I travel around the world
solving mysteries. This is a casebook of one of my
most baffling mysteries. I call it <u>The</u> <u>Mystery</u> <u>of</u>
<u>King</u> <u>Karfu</u>.

Welcome!

to the Tomb of King Karfu

Mediterranean Sea

★ Cairo

the tomb of King Karfu

Nile River

Egypt

The Mystery of King Karfu

story and pictures
by Doug Cushman

![HarperCollins] HarperCollins*Publishers*

The Stone Chicken
of King Karfu

June 24, 8:14 A.M., London, England— While finishing a little breakfast with Muggs, I receive a telegram from my good friend Professor Slagbottom.

Big Ben O'Gram
"ALWAYS ON TIME"

Seymour,

Please come to Egypt at once! My latest discovery-the Stone Chicken of King Karfu-has been stolen! I am sending two tickets for the ship the Sea Pharaoh. Meet me at the King's Tomb and help solve this mystery!

-Professor Slagbottom

Same day, 10:36 A.M. — Muggs agrees to come with me to photograph every moment of this case. After a light snack, we pack our bags and take a taxi to the dock where the <u>Sea Pharaoh</u> is waiting.

Piccadilly Taxi
Receipt

£4.00

June 24
1928

Packing List

- ✓ tie
- ✓ sandwiches
- ✓ suntan lotion
- ✓ pants
- ✓ candy bar
- ✓ fish
- ✓ chips
- ✓ underwear
- ✓ toothbrush
- ✓ hat

·Visa·

<u>Seymour Sleuth</u>
name

<u>World's Greatest Detective</u>
occupation

<u>Wombat</u>   <u>Australia</u>
species   birthplace

<u>May 4, 1888</u>
birthday

<u>June 24, 1928</u>
issue date

·Visa·

<u>Abbott Muggs</u>
name

<u>Photographer</u>
occupation

<u>mouse</u>   <u>England</u>
species   birthplace

<u>September 24, 1898</u>
birthday

<u>June 24, 1928</u>
issue date

Welcome aboard...

THE SEA PHARAOH

England

Europe

Egypt

Ticket for 1 to EGYPT ONE WAY

The Sea Pharaoh

from THE SEA PHARAOH
Ship doctor

Take 4 seasick pills daily—
Don't forget!

June 25-27, Aboard the <u>Sea Pharaoh</u> — I relax and read about Professor Slagbottom's discovery. The Stone Chicken is believed to be an important clue to the famous Lost Treasure of King Karfu. King Karfu was a gourmet cook as well as a wealthy pharaoh with many treasures. His greatest treasure was hidden in a golden box that has been missing for centuries. No one knows what the treasure is, but whoever has the Chicken may be able to find it!

June 27, 9:48 A.M., Cairo— The <u>Sea Pharaoh</u> docks in Cairo. Muggs and I ride camels to the Tomb of King Karfu. The tomb is magnificent. My camel ride is not.

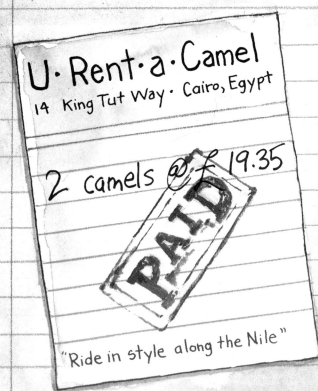

U·Rent·a·Camel
14 King Tut Way · Cairo, Egypt

2 camels @ £19.35

PAID

"Ride in style along the Nile"

The professor's camp at the tomb

Same day, 11:38 A.M., The Tomb of King Karfu — I meet my friend Professor Slagbottom. "I was in my tent late at night studying the Chicken," he explains. "I went to the food tent for a cup of tea. I was only gone a few minutes. When I returned to my tent, the Chicken was gone!"

"What about the Lost Treasure of King Karfu?" I ask. "Isn't it true that whoever stole the Chicken will be able to find the Lost Treasure?"

"That's right," says the professor. "There is a secret code written on the Chicken. I was just starting to decode it when the Chicken was stolen. We must hurry, or the thief will be able to steal the Lost Treasure too!"

Same day, 11:54 A.M. — I go to the professor's tent and view the scene of the crime. Muggs takes pictures of the clues we find.

footprint

red fish

scrap of paper

crumbs

Notes on the Suspects

Professor Slagbottom gives me a list of the others who were working near the tomb at the time of the crime. They were the only ones around the tomb that night. One of them must be the thief.

THE COOK
- has cooked for Professor Slagbottom for many years
- is usually cranky
- likes to keep to himself

DR. AMOS RAMSDELL
- expert on Egypt
- old rival of Professor Slagbottom
- visiting tomb to collect treasures for his museum

JANET SLUGG
- art student
- studied Egyptian art in school
- recently joined Professor Slagbottom's crew

Same day, lunchtime — I sit down to a small lunch and interview the cook.

"Where were you when the Chicken was stolen?" I ask him.

"I was looking through my recipes while my cookies were baking," he says. "I'm a cook, not a thief! Besides, I can't read that funny writing on the Chicken. Why would I want that old Chicken? All I want is to build my own restaurant someday."

The cook's footprint

(Note: His couscous is excellent.)

butter
salt

⅔ C couscous
1 C water
Boil water with salt. Add couscous and butter. Cover and take off heat. Let sit for 5 minutes. Serve hot.

Same day, 3:17 p.m. — I watch Janet Slugg at work. "I was sketching a mummy when the Chicken was stolen," she says. "What would I want with the Chicken anyway? Just because I studied the secret code in school doesn't make me a thief. I'm a poor artist, not a crook! I need this job to pay for my art classes." She always drinks tea and eats cookies while she works (she does not offer me any!). Could such a young artist be a thief?

Janet Slugg's footprint

Same day, 4:10 P.M. — I watch Dr. Ramsdell. He knows the tomb — and the secret code — very well. He says, "I would love to have the Stone Chicken for my museum, but I would never steal it. I'm a scholar, not a thief!" He drinks tea and eats peanut butter and celery when he works (he doesn't offer me any of those either!).

Dr. Ramsdell's footprint

Same day, 6:33 P.M.— Muggs and I go back to my tent and have a small bite to eat. I look over my notes about this baffling case. Is someone lying? Have I missed a clue?

I decide to give this case careful thought.

cookies + footprints + fish = ?

I'm hungry!

Slugg ⟶ cook?
↳   ↑
Ramsdell ?

Notes on the Clues

FOOTPRINT
- matches the cook's foot
- does not match Dr. Ramsdell's foot
- matches Janet Slugg's foot

CRUMBS
- found with the cook
- Dr. Ramsdell usually eats peanut butter and celery, doesn't leave crumbs
- found with Janet Slugg

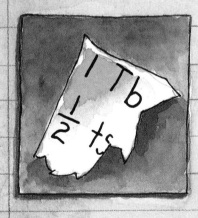

SCRAP OF PAPER
- I've seen something like it before, but I can't remember where
- Is it important?

RED FISH
- I dismiss this clue. It was a herring from the sandwich I brought for my lunch.

Notes on the Suspects

THE COOK

- foot matches print at scene of crime
- bakes cookies
- can't read secret code

DR. RAMSDELL

- foot does not match print at scene of crime
- drinks tea and eats peanut butter and celery
- can read secret code

JANET SLUGG

- foot matches print at scene of crime
- eats cookies
- can read secret code

That night, 9:47 P.M. — A message from the professor arrives at my tent.

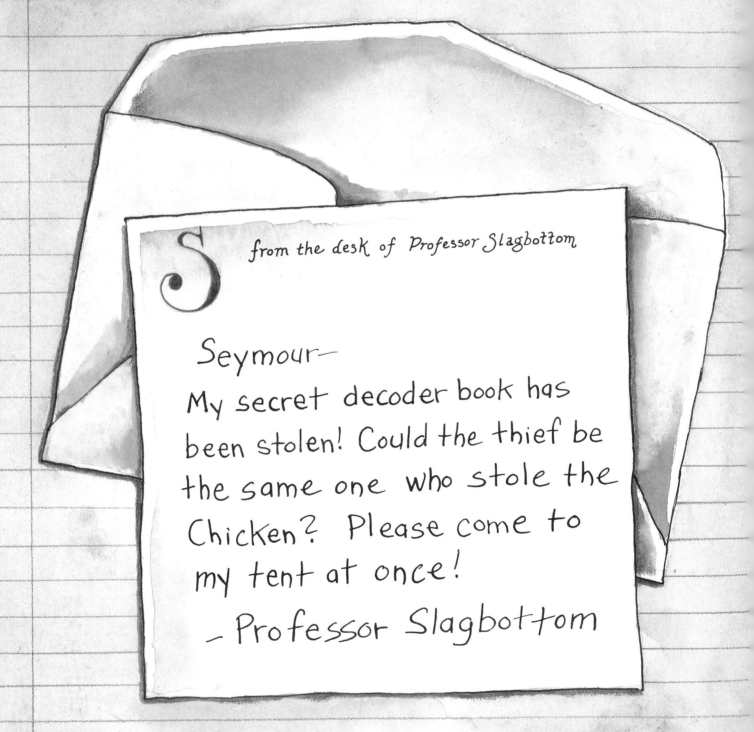

from the desk of Professor Slagbottom

Seymour—
My secret decoder book has been stolen! Could the thief be the same one who stole the Chicken? Please come to my tent at once!
— Professor Slagbottom

There is only one person who would need the decoder book. I know who the thief is!

Later that night, 9:55 P.M. — Muggs and I tell the
professor, then we all sneak up to the thief's tent.

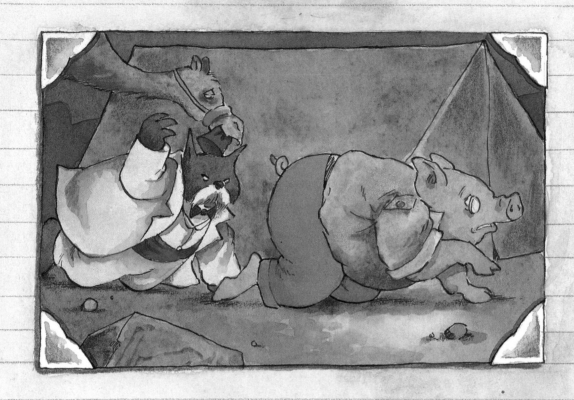

We hear a noise, but it is only my stomach growling.

We burst into the thief's tent and find...

The cook! Caught red-handed with the Stone Chicken and the decoder book!

But before we can stop him, he jumps on his camel and tries to escape.

My expert camel riding brings the crook to justice.

Same night, 11:13 P.M., Police Station — The police arrive and take the cook to jail. He confesses to the crime. The professor is happy to have the Chicken back.

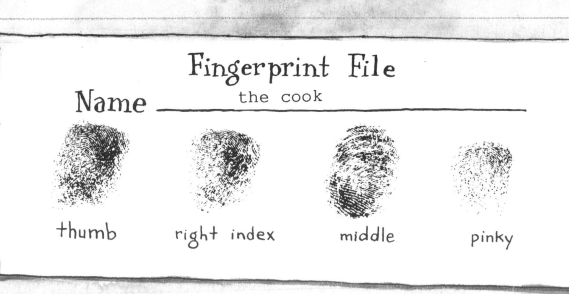

Fingerprint File

Name _____ the cook

thumb   right index   middle   pinky

Police Department
Confession Form EZ-96

I, the cook, stole the Stone Chicken of King Karfu and the professor's decoder book. I wanted to find the Lost Treasure of King Karfu so I could sell it and use the money to build my own restaurant. I am sick of cooking for Professor Slagbottom!

Signed   *The Cook*

But the case is not over yet.

June 28, 10:36 A.M., Back at the Tomb—
The professor has finished
translating the secret code on
the Chicken.

   At last we know how to find
the Lost Treasure of
King Karfu!

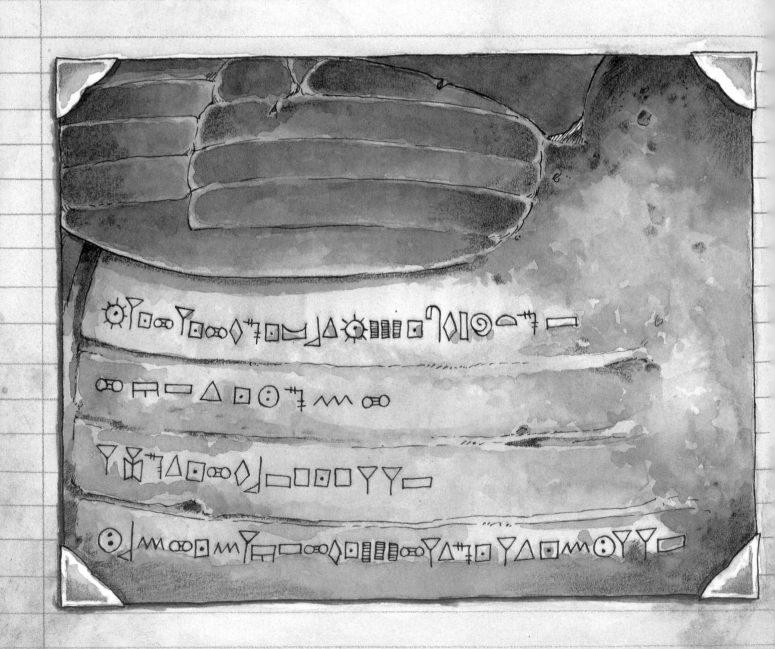

KEY TO THE SECRET CODE

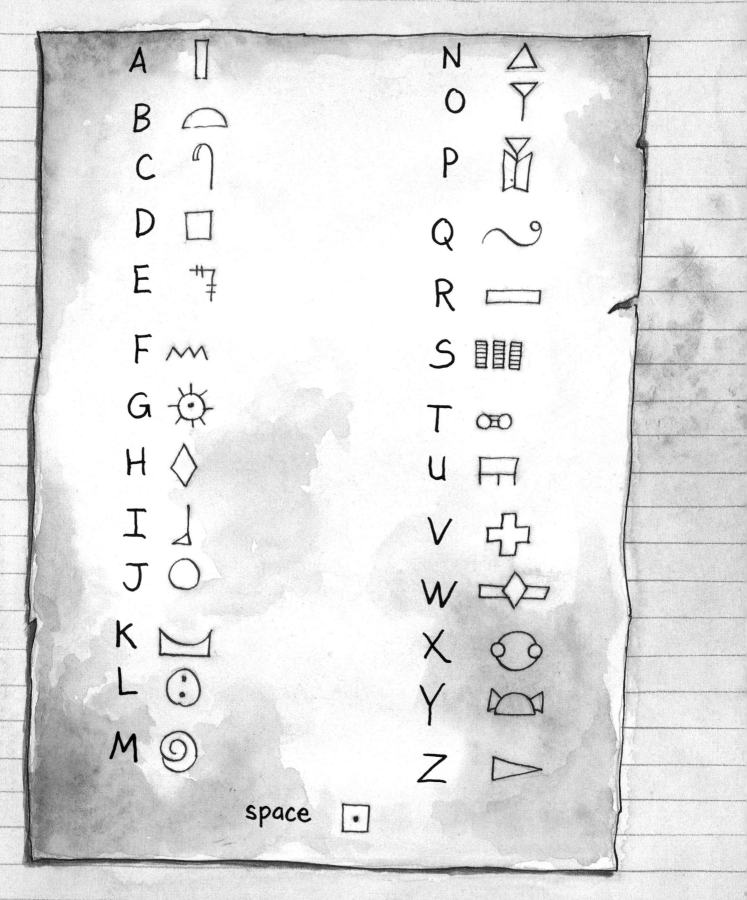

Same morning, 10:51 A.M. — Following the directions, we start at the entrance of the tomb. I graciously suggest that the professor go into the deep, dark, and spooky tunnel first while I stand guard outside. He says I should go first.

We flip a coin.

I lose.

I let Muggs go in first.

We enter the King's Chamber.

We turn left.

We open the third door.

We lift the fourth stone in the floor.

The Chicken was right! We find a golden box.
It must be the Lost Treasure!

Same day, 1:30 P.M. — The professor opens the golden box. Inside are sheets of parchment. He examines one carefully.

"What is it?" I ask.

"I believe it is a recipe," he says. "If it is, we have found what King Karfu would have treasured the most — his own secret recipes! Let's decode it and find out."

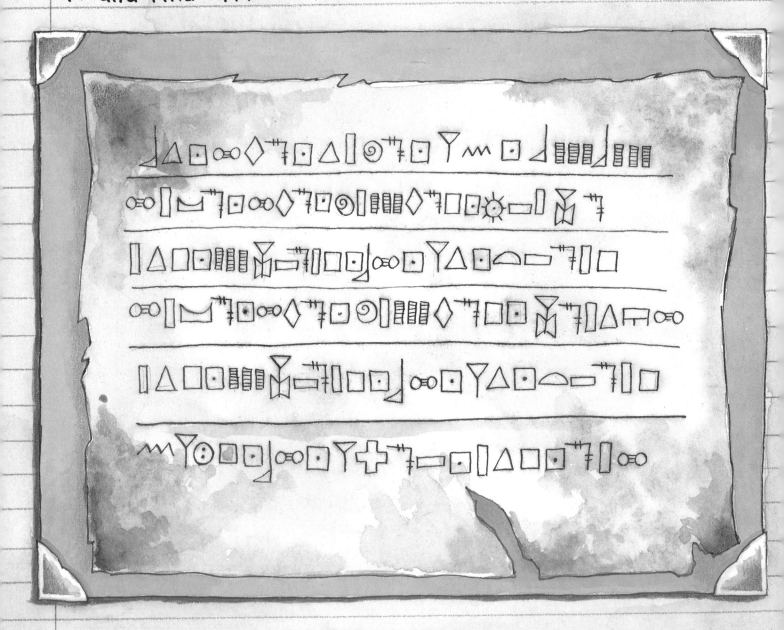

Same day, 3:26 P.M. — "Eureka!" the professor cries.
"There is no question that this is the Lost Treasure
of King Karfu — this recipe is delicious!"
    I agree with the professor. I've solved many
mysteries, but this is the tastiest one yet!

The Nile Gazette

"All the news that prints" • June 28, 1928 • Late Edition

SEYMOUR SLEUTH DOES IT AGAIN

Great Detective Solves Mystery of Stone Chicken and Helps Discover the Lost Treasure of King Karfu

(Egypt) Master detective Seymour Sleuth has solved the baffling mystery of the missing Stone Chicken of King Karfu. The thief was apprehended late last night after a high-speed camel chase. No one was injured, although one of the camels sustained a slight bruise to the knee. "All in all it was a very delicious conclusion to a troublesome case," the detective said. "There were times when I thought I couldn't do it. But we had some lucky breaks..."

The detective thanked his assistant, Abbott Muggs, for his help. "It's always a pleasure to help a great detective," said Muggs. "Besides, Seymour always knows the best places to eat."

The vile criminal was the cook of the expedition. He confessed that the

(see page 7, column 2)

For Sally Doherty who believed in the Lost Treasure from the beginning

The Mystery of King Karfu
Copyright © 1996 by Doug Cushman
Printed in the U.S.A. All rights reserved.

Library of Congress Cataloging-in-Publication Data
Cushman, Doug.
The mystery of King Karfu / story and pictures by Doug Cushman.
p. cm.
Summary: The great detective Seymour Sleuth and his assistant Muggs journey to Egypt to search for a missing stone chicken, an important clue to the Lost Treasure of King Karfu.
ISBN 0-06-024796-7. — ISBN 0-06-024797-5 (lib. bdg.)
[1. Egypt—Fiction. 2. Mystery and detective stories.]
I. Title. II. Series.
PZ7.C959My 1996
[E]—dc20

95-31064
CIP
AC

1 2 3 4 5 6 7 8 9 10
First Edition

U.S.A. TRAVEL GUIDES

ARKANSAS

BY ANN HEINRICHS • ILLUSTRATED BY MATT KANIA

The Child's World®
childsworld.com

Published by The Child's World®
1980 Lookout Drive • Mankato, MN 56003-1705
800-599-READ • www.childsworld.com

Photo Credits

Photographs ©: Shutterstock Images, cover, 1, 38
(bottom); OakleyOriginals CC2.0, 7; Rennett Stowe
CC2.0, 8; Garry Tucker/USFWS, 11; Conway Area
Chamber of Commerce, 12; Joe Arrigo/Shutterstock
Images, 15; Zach Frank/Shutterstock Images, 16;
Arkansas Department of Parks and Tourism, 19; Adam
Bartlett CC2.0, 20; Bonita R. Cheshier/Shutterstock
Images, 23; Jo Naylor CC2.0, 24; Josh Grenier CC2.0,
27; Stuart Seeger CC2.0, 28; Denis and Yulia Pogostins/
Shutterstock Images, 31; Jeff Noble CC2.0, 32; Bryan
Kemp CC2.0, 35; Rest Image/Shutterstock Images, 38
(top)

ISBN 9781503819443
LCCN 2016961121

Printing

Printed in the United States of America
PA02334

Ann Heinrichs is the author
of more than 100 books
for children and young
adults. She has also enjoyed
successful careers as a
children's book editor and
an advertising copywriter.
Ann grew up in Fort Smith,
Arkansas, and lives in
Chicago, Illinois.

About the Author
Ann Heinrichs

Matt Kania loves maps and, as a
kid, dreamed of making them. In
school he studied geography and
cartography, and today he makes
maps for a living. Matt's favorite
thing about drawing maps is
learning about the places they
represent. Many of the maps
he has created can be found in
books, magazines, videos, Web
sites, and public places.

About the
Map Illustrator
Matt Kania

*On the cover: Lawmakers meet at the Arkansas
state capitol.*

OUR ARKANSAS TRIP

ARKANSAS

What shall we do in Arkansas today? It's a great place to explore! Just look what's waiting down the road.

You'll roam through forests full of wildlife. You'll take a wild canoe ride. You'll soak in piping hot water. You'll dig for diamonds you can keep. You'll get a toad and watch it race. And you'll stuff yourself with tomatoes!

There's much more to do here. So we'd better get started! Just buckle up and hang on tight. We're off to discover Arkansas!

WELCOME TO
ARKANSAS

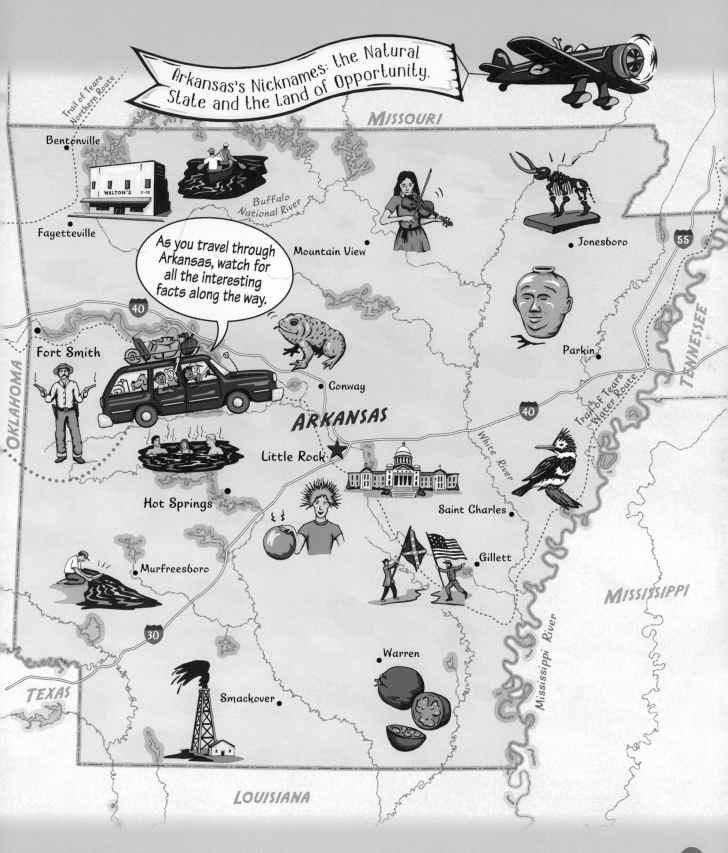

Arkansas's Nicknames: the Natural State and the Land of Opportunity.

MISSOURI

Trail of Tears Northern Route

Bentonville

WALTON'S 5-10

Fayetteville

Buffalo National River

Mountain View

Jonesboro

55

TENNESSEE

Parkin

As you travel through Arkansas, watch for all the interesting facts along the way.

40

Fort Smith

OKLAHOMA

Conway

ARKANSAS

Little Rock

40

Trail of Tears Water Route

White River

Saint Charles

Hot Springs

Murfreesboro

Gillett

30

MISSISSIPPI

Warren

Mississippi River

Smackover

TEXAS

LOUISIANA

MISSOURI

Gravette

Ozark Mountains

Buffalo City

Tyler Bend

Boston Mountains

Buffalo National River

White River

Mississippi Delta

Highest Temperature: Ozark August 10, 1936 120°F (49°C)

OKLAHOMA

Ozark

Arkansas River

Magazine Mountain

Lowest Temperature: Gravette February 13, 1905 −29°F (−34°C)

TENNESSEE

Ouachita Mountains

We'll see signs along the river. They'll tell us what the river conditions are at certain points. We have to be expert boaters to go in where the river flows swiftly.

Mississippi River

MISSISSIPPI

The Buffalo River was the nation's first national river. Laws protect national rivers from dams and other construction. The Buffalo River begins in the Boston Mountains. Then it flows into the White River near Buffalo City.

Forests cover Arkansas's southern plains.

The Ozarks lie mainly in southern Missouri. Arkansas boasts the highest and most rugged part of the Ozarks. It's called the Boston Mountains.

Ouachita River

TEXAS

A big park runs alongside the Buffalo River. Its main visitors' center is at Tyler Bend.

LOUISIANA

HIGHEST AND LOWEST POINTS
HIGHEST: Magazine Mountain at 2,753 feet (839 m)
LOWEST: Ouachita River along the southern border at 55 feet (17 m)

CANOEING THE BUFFALO NATIONAL RIVER

Wahoo! What a wild ride! You'll love canoeing down the Buffalo National River. Some sections are smooth, but some are rough. Hang on tight!

This river winds through the Ozark Mountains. The Ozarks cover north and northwest Arkansas. They slope down toward the Arkansas River. This river flows southeast across the state. It empties into the great Mississippi River. The Ouachita Mountains reach into west-central Arkansas. Many lakes and streams sparkle among the mountains. Hot-water springs bubble up from underground, too. The Mississippi River forms Arkansas's eastern border. Land along the river is very fertile. It's often called the Mississippi Delta.

Canoe down the Buffalo National River. If you need a break, take a dip in the cool water!

IN HOT WATER IN HOT SPRINGS

Suppose you say you're in hot water. What does that mean?

It means you're in big trouble! But not in Hot Springs. Here, it means you're taking a healthful bath!

Hot springs is a national park. The water gushes from 47 underground springs. It is pumped into buildings along **Bathhouse** Row.

Try a nice, hot soak. But there's much more to do around here. Hot Springs National Park covers a big area. Hike through its forested mountains. Just don't get too close to a steep mountainside. You'll be in hot water!

Lamar Bathhouse is one of eight old bathhouses that you can find in Hot Springs.

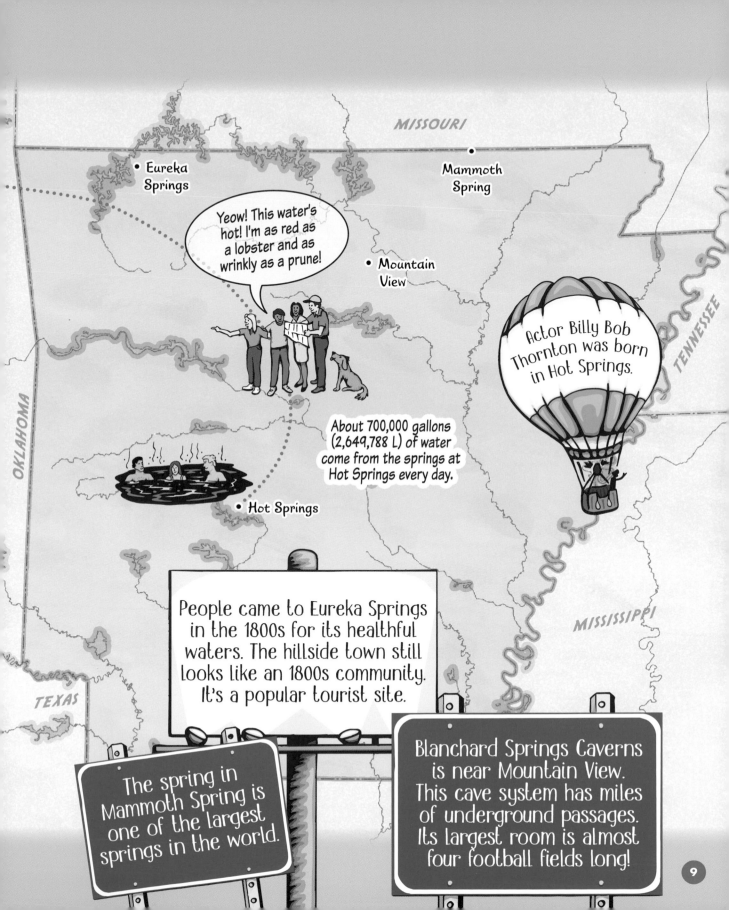

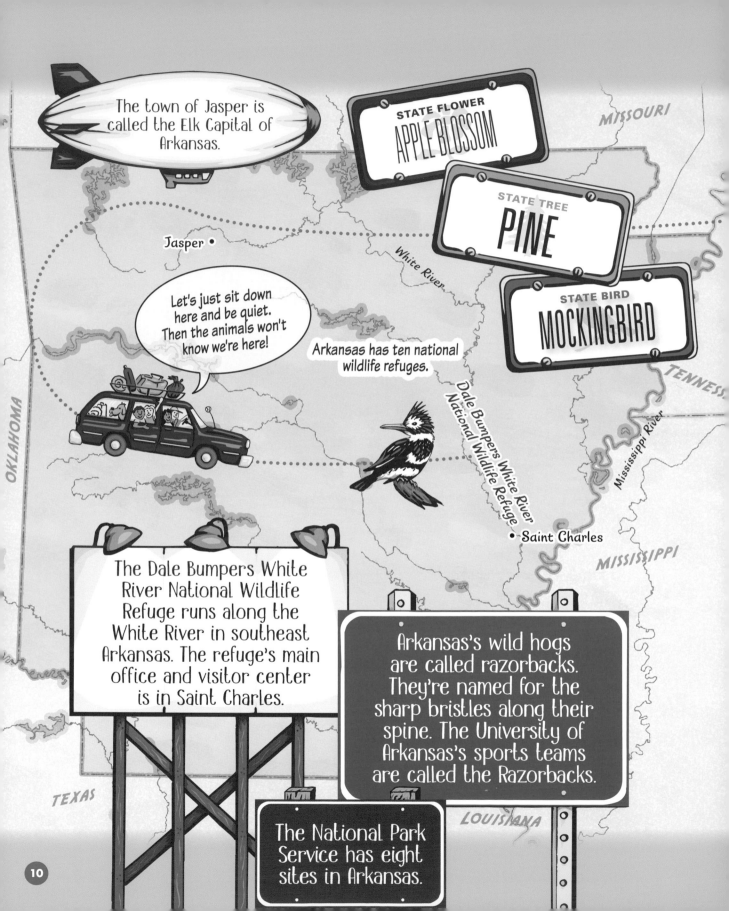

The town of Jasper is called the Elk Capital of Arkansas.

STATE FLOWER
APPLE BLOSSOM

STATE TREE
PINE

STATE BIRD
MOCKINGBIRD

Jasper •

White River

Let's just sit down here and be quiet. Then the animals won't know we're here!

Arkansas has ten national wildlife refuges.

Dale Bumpers White River National Wildlife Refuge

Mississippi River

• Saint Charles

MISSOURI

TENNESSEE

MISSISSIPPI

OKLAHOMA

TEXAS

LOUISIANA

The Dale Bumpers White River National Wildlife Refuge runs along the White River in southeast Arkansas. The refuge's main office and visitor center is in Saint Charles.

Arkansas's wild hogs are called razorbacks. They're named for the sharp bristles along their spine. The University of Arkansas's sports teams are called the Razorbacks.

The National Park Service has eight sites in Arkansas.

EXPLORING WHITE RIVER NATIONAL WILDLIFE REFUGE

Creep through the Dale Bumpers White River National Wildlife Refuge. You're bound to see lots of animals. When's the best time to look for them? In the early morning or late afternoon. Animals roam around when the sun's not too hot.

Look by the river or around a pond. Animals go there to drink. You'll see deer, beavers, foxes, and wild hogs. You might even spot alligators or bears. You'll see plenty of turtles, lizards, and frogs. Kingfishers fish by the water, and ducks swim past you. Eagles and hawks soar high above you. They're looking for small animals to eat!

A variety of amphibians can be found at the Wildlife Refuge.

TOAD SUCK DAZE IN CONWAY

Pick out a toad from the toad pen. Or bring your own toad if you like. Then line up for the Toad Races. It's time for Toad Suck Daze!

This is a fun festival in Conway. It offers pet shows and music. There's a Baby Crawl race. And there's the Tour de Toad bike race. Don't miss the pancake breakfast!

No frogs may enter—only toads. What's the difference? Toads have rough, dry, bumpy skin. But frogs have smooth, moist skin. Happy hopping!

Grab a toad and head for the race in Conway!

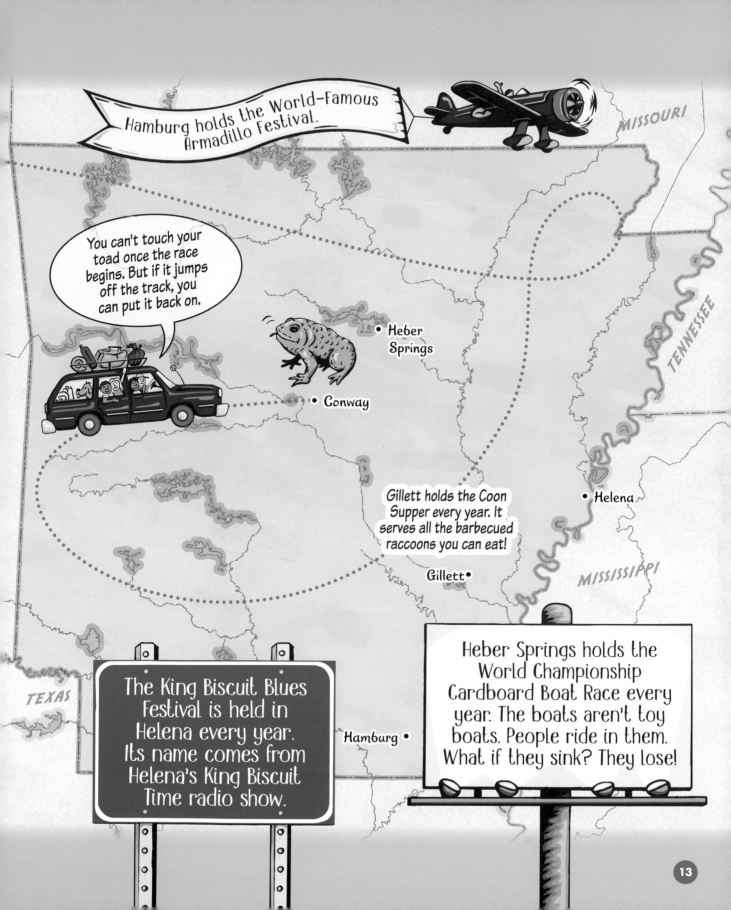

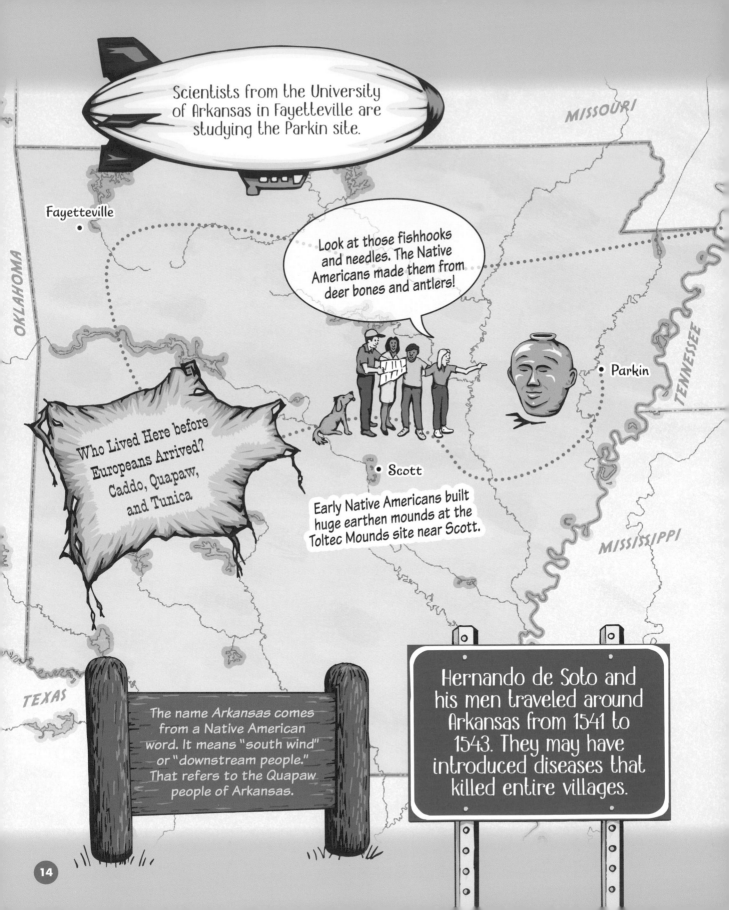

Who lived in Arkansas 1,000 years ago? Just visit Parkin, and you'll see. A Native American community lived there from about 1000 to 1600 AD. A deep ditch surrounded their village for safety. They made pottery jugs molded to look like human faces. They grew corn, beans, and other crops.

Hernando de Soto arrived in Arkansas in 1541. He was a Spanish explorer. De Soto visited a village he called Casqui. **Historians** believe the Parkin site is that village. They think the village never had more than 2,000 people.

You can visit Parkin Archeological State Park. You'll see the Native Americans' art, pottery, and tools. And you'll watch **archaeologists** dig for ancient objects.

*Archeological is the preferred spelling of the Parkin Archeological State Park.

Parkin has Native American artifacts that are over 1,000 years old.

Want to walk through 300 years of history? Just stroll through Arkansas Post. It was Arkansas's first European settlement. Frenchman Henri de Tonti founded it in 1686. He started trading goods with the Quapaw Native American tribe.

Over time, the Frenchmen and Quapaw became friends. They married one another and fought on the same side in wars.

The United States took over present-day Arkansas in 1803 and the Quapaw were eventually forced onto reservations. Arkansas Territory was established in 1819. By then, Arkansas Post was a busy river port. It became the new territory's capital.

Arkansas Post was destroyed during the U.S. Civil War (1861–1865). Northern and Southern states were fighting over states's rights and slavery. Arkansas was on the Confederate side. Northern states formed the Union side. In the end, the Union won the war.

Arkansas Post was the first European settlement in Arkansas. Visit this state park to learn about its history!

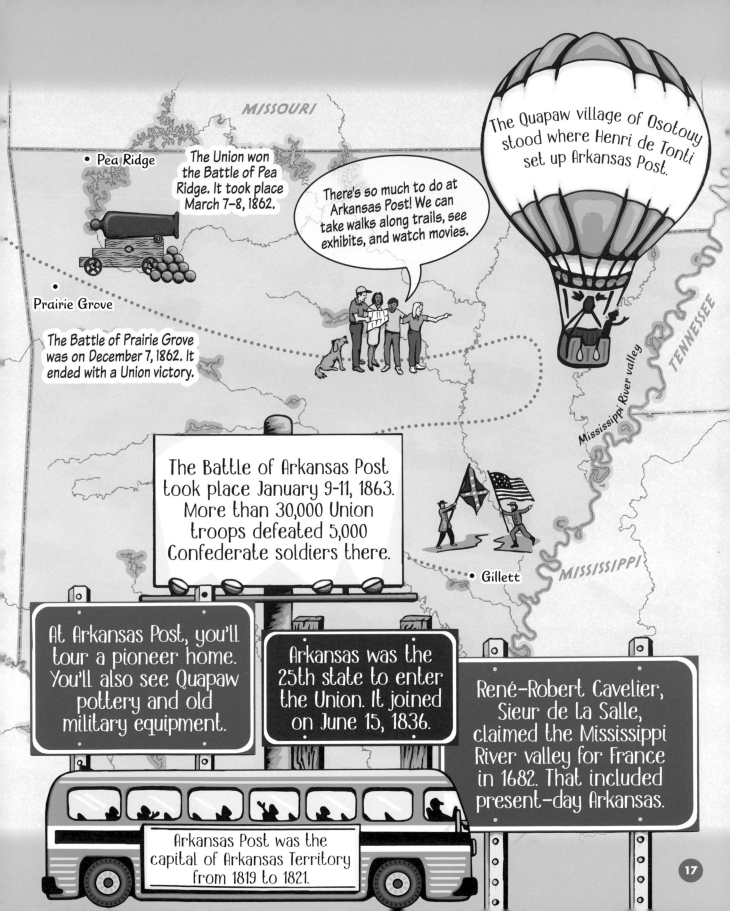

MISSOURI

Pea Ridge

The Union won the Battle of Pea Ridge. It took place March 7–8, 1862.

There's so much to do at Arkansas Post! We can take walks along trails, see exhibits, and watch movies.

The Quapaw village of Osotouy stood where Henri de Tonti set up Arkansas Post.

Prairie Grove

The Battle of Prairie Grove was on December 7, 1862. It ended with a Union victory.

TENNESSEE

Mississippi River valley

Mississippi

The Battle of Arkansas Post took place January 9-11, 1863. More than 30,000 Union troops defeated 5,000 Confederate soldiers there.

Gillett

MISSISSIPPI

At Arkansas Post, you'll tour a pioneer home. You'll also see Quapaw pottery and old military equipment.

Arkansas was the 25th state to enter the Union. It joined on June 15, 1836.

René-Robert Cavelier, Sieur de La Salle, claimed the Mississippi River valley for France in 1682. That included present-day Arkansas.

Arkansas Post was the capital of Arkansas Territory from 1819 to 1821.

The Arkansas State Fiddler's Championship is held at Ozark Folk Center in Mountain View.

• Fayetteville
• Hogeye

Snowball •

Mountain View

Actor Mary Steenburgen was born in Newport.

• Newport

• Fort Smith

In 2016, 2,988,248 people lived in Arkansas. It's the 33rd-largest state by population.

Watch that wood-carver! He's carving an old man's face onto that walking stick!

• Greasy Corner

★ Little Rock

OKLAHOMA

TENNESSEE

MISSISSIPPI

Country music singer Johnny Cash was born in Kingsland.

• Kingsland

You'll see people working at more than 20 crafts in the Ozark Folk Center's craft village.

Folk singer and songwriter Jimmy Driftwood was born near Mountain View.

Population of Largest Cities

Little Rock	197,992
Fort Smith	88,194
Fayetteville	82,830

Arkansas has towns named Hogeye, Greasy Corner, and Snowball!

PIONEER LIFE IN MOUNTAIN VIEW

Suppose you lived way up in the mountains. How would you get soap, toys, or clothes? You'd make them!

That's what Arkansas **pioneers** did in the 1800s. They settled in the rugged mountains. They were far from towns or stores. Their skills helped them stay alive.

Mountain View preserves this way of life. Just visit the Ozark Folk Center State Park. You'll see people making brooms, pottery, and soap. Some are making dolls, candles, or musical instruments. Fiddlers and banjo players strike up tunes. And everyone's happy to explain what they're doing.

Children will learn what pioneer life was really like at the Ozark Folk Center!

LAW AND ORDER IN FORT SMITH

Glance around the old courtroom. You can almost hear the judge's booming voice. Look at the old jail cells. Many outlaws spent their last days here.

You're touring the Fort Smith National Historic Site. Judge Isaac Parker ruled over the court here. He was known for his harsh sentences.

Fort Smith is right on the Oklahoma border. In the 1800s, Oklahoma was Indian Territory before the U.S. government forced Native Americans onto reservations. Outlaws also roamed this land. But some got caught. Judge Parker's job was to decide their fate.

Many outlaws received their sentences from Judge Isaac Parker at the Fort Smith Courthouse.

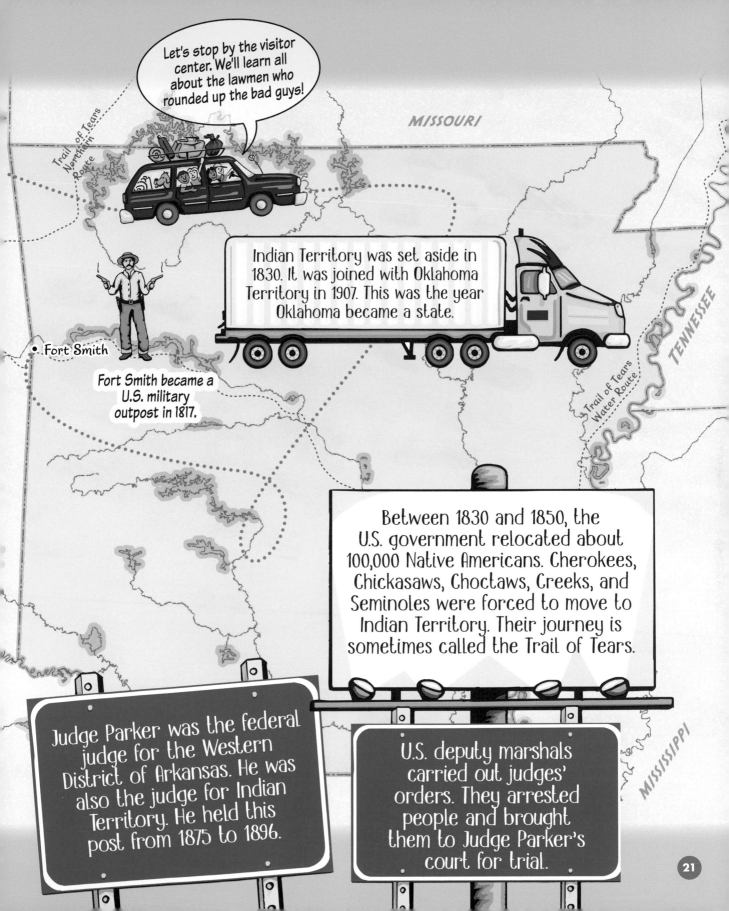

Today, it's easy to get gasoline for cars. We just drive to a gas station. But things were different in the 1920s. Cars were a fairly new invention. And the oil **industry** was new, too. (Petroleum, or oil, is made into gasoline.)

You'll learn about these days in Smackover. Just visit the Arkansas Museum of Natural Resources! Outdoors, you'll see working oil **derricks**. Indoors, you'll see old cars and gas-station pumps.

Oil was discovered in El Dorado in 1921. Smackover's first oil well opened in 1922. Thousands of people swarmed in to get jobs. It was an exciting time!

This old crooked ladder is attached to a metal oil derrick.

WALMART'S BIRTHPLACE IN BENTONVILLE

Have you ever been to Walmart? These stores are named after Sam Walton. In 1950, he opened a little store in Bentonville. Now there are Walmart stores all over the world!

You can visit Walton's first Bentonville store. It's called the Walmart Museum now. It's a museum of Walmart history. You'll see Sam's old office and pickup truck. And you'll see some Ol' Roy Dog Food. It was named after Walton's dog!

Stores such as Walmart are busy in Arkansas. So are factories. Food products are the state's major factory goods. Many factories make paper and metal goods, too.

You can still visit Sam Walton's first store in Bentonville!

MISSOURI

TENNESSEE

MISSISSIPPI

TEXAS

OKLAHOMA

Bentonville
Rogers
Springdale
Fayetteville

WALTON'S 5-10

Hey, Sparky! Wouldn't it be cool to have dog food named after you?

Fortune magazine listed Walmart as the highest-earning store of its kind in 2016.

What's Made in Arkansas? Food products, fabricated metal products, and paper products

What's Mined in Arkansas? Natural gas, petroleum, bromine, and crushed stone

Walmart has more than 5,200 stores in the United States. It also has more than 6,000 stores in other countries.

You can visit Terra Studios in Fayetteville. There you'll watch glassblowing and learn to make pottery.

Forbes magazine listed Sam Walton as the richest man in the United States from 1985 to 1988. He died in 1992.

Potlatch Corporation is in Warren. It makes lumber, paper, and other wood products.

Warren

Springdale is the home of Tyson Foods. This company owns one of the world's largest chicken-processing plants.

The first store with the name Walmart opened in Rogers in 1962.

25

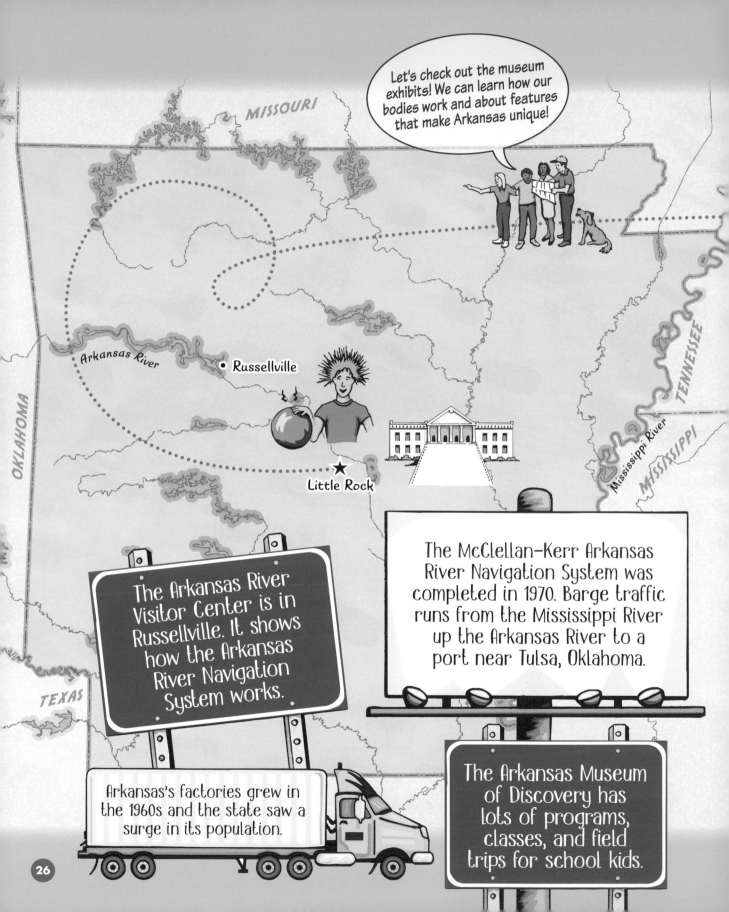

Let's check out the museum exhibits! We can learn how our bodies work and about features that make Arkansas unique!

MISSOURI

OKLAHOMA

Arkansas River

• Russellville

★ Little Rock

TEXAS

TENNESSEE

Mississippi River

MISSISSIPPI

The Arkansas River Visitor Center is in Russellville. It shows how the Arkansas River Navigation System works.

The McClellan–Kerr Arkansas River Navigation System was completed in 1970. Barge traffic runs from the Mississippi River up the Arkansas River to a port near Tulsa, Oklahoma.

Arkansas's factories grew in the 1960s and the state saw a surge in its population.

The Arkansas Museum of Discovery has lots of programs, classes, and field trips for school kids.

LITTLE ROCK'S ARKANSAS MUSEUM OF DISCOVERY

Use your body's energy to turn lights on. Feel electricity make your hair stand straight out. Meet creepy, crawly bugs and even hold some. See what the dentist sees inside your mouth. You're exploring the Arkansas Museum of Discovery in Little Rock!

Scientific discoveries helped Arkansas grow. Scientists and engineers developed better farm equipment. Farms then needed fewer workers. People moved to cities for factory work.

Waterway engineers improved the Arkansas River, too. Then large chains of **barges** could use the river. This brought new business to Arkansas's river ports. Look for barges when you cross the Arkansas River!

There are many things to learn at the Museum of Discovery!

THE STATE CAPITOL IN LITTLE ROCK

Does the Little Rock capitol building look familiar to you? It should. It looks like the U.S. Capitol in Washington, DC. That's where the nation's lawmakers meet. Sometimes moviemakers want to show the U.S. Capitol. They film the Arkansas capitol instead!

Many state government offices are in the capitol. Arkansas's state government has three branches. One branch makes the laws. Its members belong to the General Assembly. They meet in the capitol. A second branch carries out the laws. It's headed by the governor. Judges make up the third branch of government. They decide whether someone has broken the law.

The capitol building took 16 years to build.

Stuttgart is home to the Museum of the Arkansas Grand Prairie. It shows how Arkansas became the nation's top rice producer.

They've got turtle races at the tomato festival. Turtles love tomatoes. They have to be fast to get the juiciest ones!

• Tontitown

• Lincoln

Mountain View •

Weiner •

• Altus
• Clarksville

The state fair is held in Little Rock in early autumn each year.

OKLAHOMA

TENNESSEE

MISSISSIPPI

★ Little Rock

Stuttgart •

Warren is in Bradley County. Farmers there grow pink tomatoes: Bradleys and Arkansas Travelers. Look for them in farmers' markets.

Some Arkansas Farm Product Festivals
Apple Festival (Lincoln)
Bean Festival (Mountain View)
Grape Festival (Tontitown)
Peach Festival (Clarksville)
Rice Festival (Weiner)
Watermelon Festival (Hope)
Wine Festival (Altus)

• Hope

Warren •

TEXAS

LOUISIANA

What Does Arkansas Raise?
Broilers (chickens), beef cattle, cotton, and rice

The pink tomato is Arkansas's official state fruit and vegetable. Tomatoes are actually fruits. But people use them as vegetables.

30

WARREN'S PINK TOMATO FESTIVAL

Do you like tomatoes? Then try the tomato-eating contest. Do you have a dog? You might want to enter it in the cutest dog contest. Are you still hungry? Then belly up to the all-tomato lunch. You're at the Pink Tomato Festival in Warren!

Tomatoes are a delicious Arkansas product. But rice and soybeans are the leading crops. No other state grows more rice. Arkansas is a top chicken state, too. Chickens bring in the most farm income. Many farmers raise beef cattle, hogs, and turkeys. Wild turkeys live in the woods. Want a turkey to come running? Then practice your turkey calls. Turkey calling is a fine art in Arkansas!

Arkansas takes pride in its pink tomatoes.

DIGGING FOR DIAMONDS IN MURFREESBORO

Bring your bucket and shovel. Then start digging for diamonds. What if you find one? Finders keepers!

You're diamond hunting at the Crater of Diamonds State Park in Murfreesboro. It's the nation's only diamond-mining site. Thousands of diamonds have been found there. Most are tiny, but some are huge.

Diamonds aren't sparkly when you dig them up. They're sort of dark and greasy looking. How can you tell a diamond from gravel? Park workers help you. They teach you what raw diamonds look like. And they show you how to search. Good luck!

Come dig for diamonds in Arkansas!

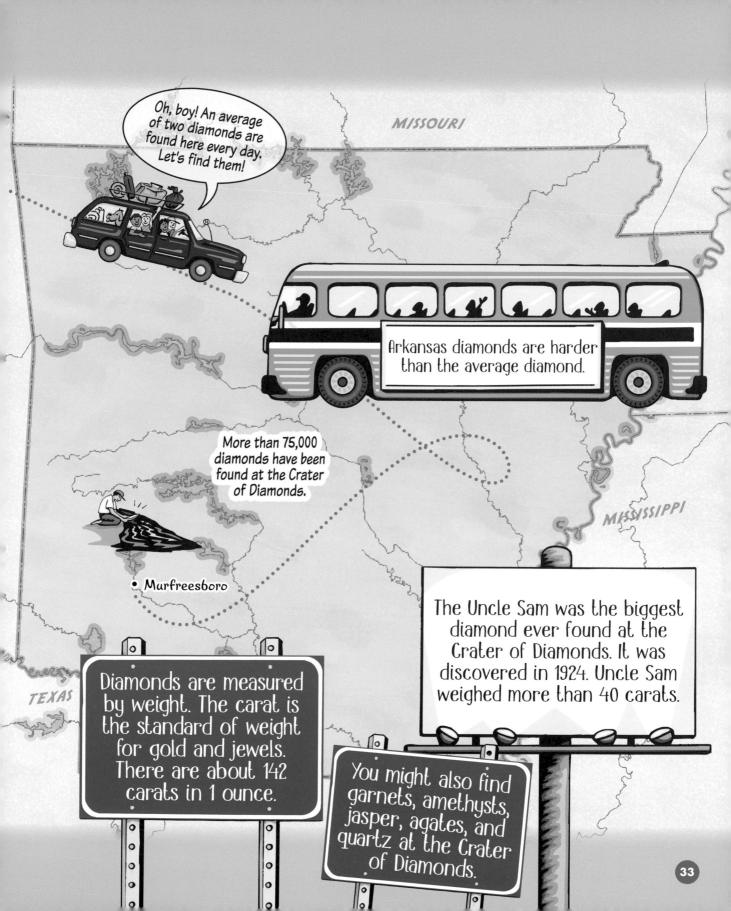

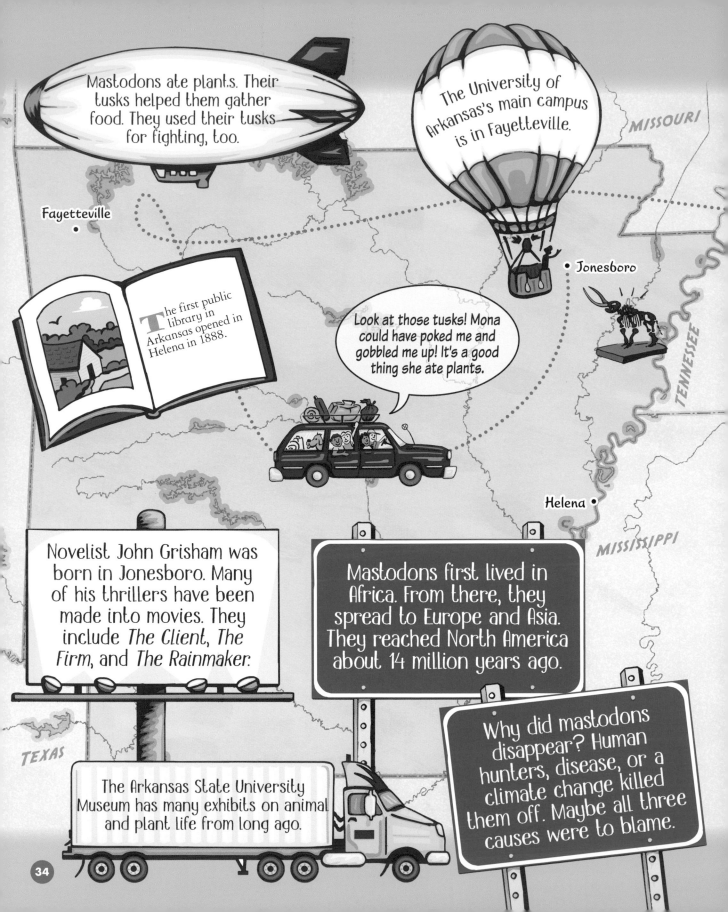

MEET MONA THE MASTODON

W atch out! She's pretty tall. In fact, you barely come up to her knees. She's Mona the mastodon!

Mastodons are relatives of elephants. They lived millions of years ago. They had shaggy coats and long, curved tusks. Mona is a copy of a real mastodon skeleton. You'll find her in Jonesboro. She's in the Arkansas State University Museum.

Arkansas was a great place for mastodons. They've been found in 20 sites there. Mastodons disappeared about 10,000 years ago. Now, take a long look at Mona.

Are you glad or sad that mastodons are gone?

Mastodons lived millions of years ago and once called Arkansas home.

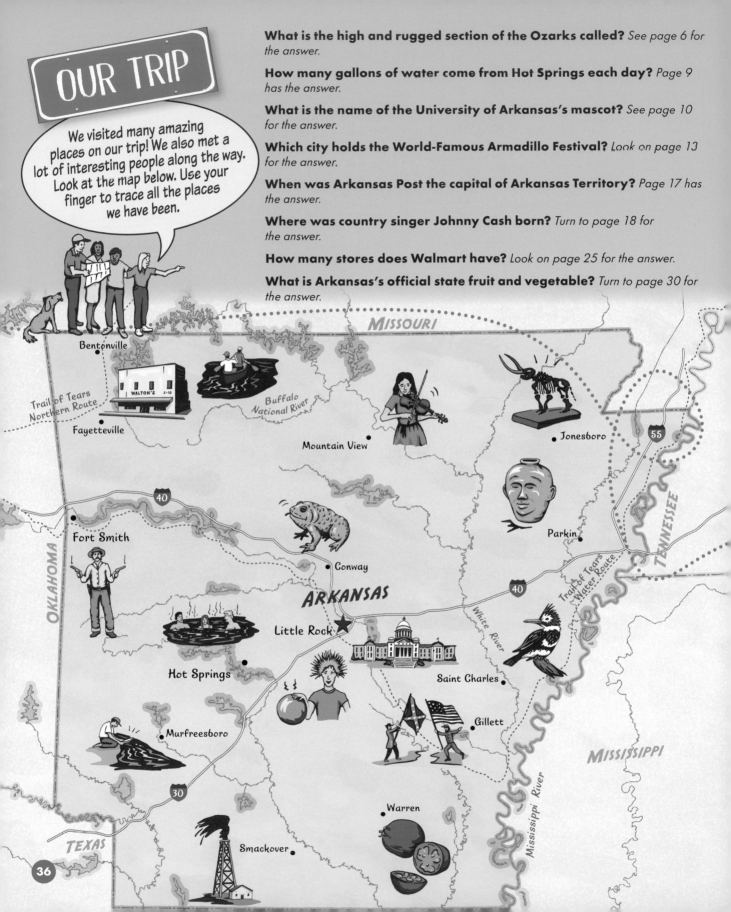

OUR TRIP

We visited many amazing places on our trip! We also met a lot of interesting people along the way. Look at the map below. Use your finger to trace all the places we have been.

What is the high and rugged section of the Ozarks called? *See page 6 for the answer.*

How many gallons of water come from Hot Springs each day? *Page 9 has the answer.*

What is the name of the University of Arkansas's mascot? *See page 10 for the answer.*

Which city holds the World-Famous Armadillo Festival? *Look on page 13 for the answer.*

When was Arkansas Post the capital of Arkansas Territory? *Page 17 has the answer.*

Where was country singer Johnny Cash born? *Turn to page 18 for the answer.*

How many stores does Walmart have? *Look on page 25 for the answer.*

What is Arkansas's official state fruit and vegetable? *Turn to page 30 for the answer.*

MISSOURI

Bentonville

Trail of Tears Northern Route

WALTON'S 5-10

Buffalo National River

Fayetteville

Mountain View

Jonesboro

55

TENNESSEE

40

Fort Smith

Parkin

Conway

ARKANSAS

40

White River

Trail of Tears Water Route

OKLAHOMA

Little Rock

Saint Charles

Hot Springs

Gillett

Murfreesboro

Warren

MISSISSIPPI

30

Mississippi River

TEXAS

Smackover

36

STATE SYMBOLS

State beverage: Milk

State bird: Mockingbird

State flower: Apple blossom

State folk dance: Square dance

State fruit and vegetable:
Vine ripe pink tomato

State gem: Diamond

State insect: Honeybee

State mammal: White-tailed deer

State mineral: Quartz crystal

State musical instrument: Fiddle

State rock: Bauxite

State tree: Pine

STATE SONG

"ARKANSAS"

Arkansas has two official state songs. They are "Arkansas (You Run Deep in Me)" by Wayland Holyfield and "Oh, Arkansas" by Terry Rose and Gary Klaff. Arkansas also has an official state historical song, "The Arkansas Traveler." The official state anthem is "Arkansas" by Eva Ware Barnett. Words and music by Eva Ware Barnett

I am thinking tonight of the Southland,
Of the home of my childhood days,
Where I roamed through the woods and the meadows
By the mill and the brook that plays;
Where the roses are in bloom
And the sweet magnolia, too,
Where the jasmine is white
And the fields are violet blue,
There a welcome awaits all her children
Who have wandered afar from home.

Chorus:
Arkansas, Arkansas, 'tis a name dear,
'Tis the place I call "home, sweet home";

Arkansas, Arkansas, I salute thee,
From thy shelter no more I'll roam.

'Tis a land full of joy and of sunshine,
Rich in pearls and in diamonds rare,
Full of hope, faith, and love for the stranger,
Who may pass 'neath her portals fair;
There the rice fields are full,
And the cotton, corn, and hay,
There the fruits of the field,
Bloom in the winter months and May,
'Tis the land that I love, first of all, dear,
And to her let us all give cheer.

(Chorus)

That was a great trip! We have traveled all over Arkansas. There are a few places that we didn't have time for, though. Next time, we plan to visit the Arkansas Alligator Farm and Petting Zoo in Hot Springs. They have over 300 alligators. Some are up to 10 feet (3.0m) long! Visitors can also see deer, goats, wolves, and peacocks.

FAMOUS PEOPLE

Angelou, Maya (1928-2014), author and poet

Bates, Daisy Lee Gatson (1914-1999), civil rights activist

Campbell, Glen (1936-), singer, guitarist, and songwriter

Cash, Johnny (1932-2003), singer and songwriter

Cleaver, Eldridge (1935-1998), civil rights activist and author

Clinton, Bill (1946-), 42nd U.S. president

Fletcher, John Gould (1886-1950), poet

Fulbright, J. William (1905-1995), politician and educator

Green, David Gordon (1975-), film director

Grisham, John (1955-), novelist

Huckabee, Mike (1955-), former governor of Arkansas

Jones, E. Fay (1921-2004), architect and designer

Joplin, Scott (1868-1917), composer and pianist

Ladd, Alan (1913-1964), actor

Liston, Sonny (1932-1970), professional boxer

MacArthur, Douglas (1880-1964), World War II general

Martin, Mark (1959-), NASCAR driver

Pippen, Scottie (1965-), basketball player

Saracen (ca. 1735-1832), Quapaw American Native chief

Stone, Edward Durell (1902-1978), architect

Thornton, Billy Bob (1955-), actor

Walton, Sam (1918-1992), founder of Walmart

Wood, Audrey (1930-), children's book author and illustrator

WORDS TO KNOW

archaeologists (ar-kee-oh-LOJ-ists) people who study human history by looking at artifacts and physical remains

barges (BAR-jez) long boats with flat bottoms

bathhouse (BATH-houss) a building where people take healthful baths

derricks (DER-iks) towers with equipment for drilling into the ground for oil

historians (hi-STOR-ree-unz) people who study events in history

industry (IN-duh-stree) a type of business

pioneers (pye-uh-NEERZ) people who settle in a new area

State flag

State seal

TO LEARN MORE

IN THE LIBRARY

Marsh, Carole. *I'm Reading about Arkansas*. Peachtree City, GA: Gallopade International, 2014.

Oachs, Emily Rose. *Arkansas: The Natural State*. Minneapolis, MN: Bellwether, 2014.

O'Brien, Cynthia. *Explore with Sieur de la Salle*. New York, NY: Crabtree, 2015.

Stuckey, Rachel. *Explore with Hernando de Soto*. New York, NY: Crabtree, 2017.

Zabludoff, Marc. *Mastodon*. Tarrytown, NY: Marshall Cavendish Benchmark, 2011.

ON THE WEB

Visit our Web site for links about Arkansas:
childsworld.com/links

Note to Parents, Teachers, and Librarians: We routinely verify our Web links to make sure they are safe and active sites. So encourage your readers to check them out!

PLACES TO VISIT OR CONTACT

Arkansas Department of Parks and Tourism
arkansas.com
One Capitol Mall
Little Rock, AR 72201
501/682-7777
For more information about traveling in Arkansas

Arkansas History Commission
ark-ives.com
One Capitol Mall
Little Rock, AR 72201
501/682-6900
For more information about the history of Arkansas

Arkansas covers 53,179 square miles (137,773 sq km). It's the 29th-largest state in size.

INDEX

Bye, Land of Opportunity. We had a great time. We'll come back soon!